W9-DFW-726

Fire-Breathers' Academy

by Tina Gagliardi   illustrated by Patrick Girouard

Carly's
DRAGON
DAYS

magic
wagon

visit us at www.abdopublishing.com

Text by Tina Gagliardi
Illustrations by Patrick Girouard
Edited by Nadia Higgins and Jill Sherman
Interior layout and design by Nicole Brecke
Cover design by Nicole Brecke

Library of Congress Cataloging-in-Publication Data

Gagliardi, Tina.
  Fire-breathers' academy / by Tina Gagliardi ; illustrated by Patrick Girouard.
     p. cm. — (Carly's dragon days)
  ISBN 978-1-60270-595-1
  [1. Dragons—Fiction.] I. Girouard, Patrick, ill. II. Title.
  PZ7.G1242Fin 2009
  [E]—dc22

                              2008035938

Far away, on the other side of the world and a little to the north, there is a school high above the woods.

Fire-Breathers' Academy

In each class, row after row of desks are filled with young dragons, ready to learn. The students are all the same age, but some are tiny and some are huge. Some are green. Some are red. Some are even purple.

Carly was an ordinary green dragon, not too big and not too tiny. She sat in her assigned seat behind Abigail, a pretty purple dragon.

As soon as the teacher, Mrs. Longhorn, asked a question, Abigail raised her hand. As she did, she stretched her wings straight out.

"I can't see!" Carly complained.

Abigail turned around and snorted. "Maybe you should stop complaining and answer a question yourself," she said.

Carly sighed. Too bad Abigail wasn't as pretty on the inside as she was on the outside.

Each afternoon, Carly's third-grade class had dragon lessons.

For most dragons, their true dragon abilities really began to shine at eight years old. Carly's classmates were starting to discover their talents.

Everyone always bragged about how scary they were. But Carly certainly didn't feel scary. She wondered what her talent could be.

Carly thought dragon lessons were a pain. She could never get things quite right.

She was good at hiding treasure. But she could never remember where she put it.

She could never aim fire where she was supposed to, either.

Carly didn't understand why she had to steal treasure or burn things, anyway. All she ever wanted to do was fly, fly, fly. She loved the feeling of the wind through her horns as she sped through the trees.

At recess one day, some of the older students were playing Knights and Dragons. The third graders watched with excitement as the older dragons chased each other.

A large dragon named Kevin zoomed past Carly and her friend Randy.

"Wow!" said Randy. "Kevin is so fast. I bet he'll be the first to capture a knight after graduation!"

Carly wanted to join in so badly, she could barely keep her wings from flapping.

When Carly got home, she flopped down on her bed and sighed. She was sick of dragon lessons.

Who would understand how she felt? Certainly none of her dragon friends.

Carly imagined a human. A human girl, a girl named . . . Carly thought for a moment. "Gretchen!" she cried. Gretchen would understand.

"I do understand," a sweet voice said.

Carly couldn't believe it! The human friend she'd imagined was sitting right next to her. Carly and Gretchen spent the rest of the night becoming best friends.

The next day, Carly took her imaginary friend to school.

They worked on spelling lists together. Gretchen taught Carly how to count on five fingers, and Carly showed her how to count on three claws.

At recess, Carly and Gretchen ran to watch the Knights and Dragons game.

"Go Kevin!" the two friends cheered.

Suddenly, Kevin swatted at a dragonfly. He swerved sideways—right into the side of the school!

Kevin's friends rushed him to the nurse's office.

"**H**ey Carly," a fourth grader yelled. "Do you want to take Kevin's spot in the game?"

"Uh . . . Ummm." Carly didn't know what to say.

"You can do it!" Gretchen whispered in her ear.

"Carly! Carly!" cheered the other third graders—except for one.

Carly heard Abigail mutter, "I bet she'll fly into a tree."

"Oh, just ignore her," said Gretchen.

A sixth-grade dragon was chosen to be the knight. With Gretchen cheering her on, Carly took a deep breath and flew into the game. One by one, the sixth grader tagged every dragon in the game, except for Carly.

Carly weaved confidently through the trees. Carly realized she didn't have to be scary. She was the fastest dragon in the entire school!

As she swooped down, she heard Randy say, "I bet Carly will be the first one to catch a real knight!" And everyone agreed, even Abigail.

What do you recall from Carly's Dragon Days?

1. What grade is Carly in?

2. How does Abigail annoy Carly in class?

3. What game do the older dragons play at recess?

4. How does Gretchen help Carly?

5. What is Carly really good at?

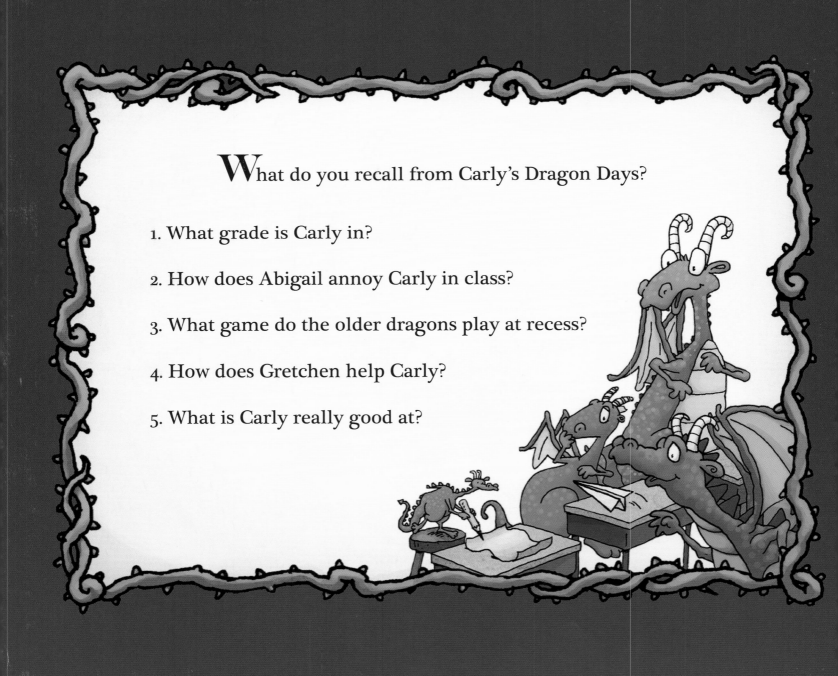